BRIGHT and EARLY BOOKS for BEGINNING Beginners

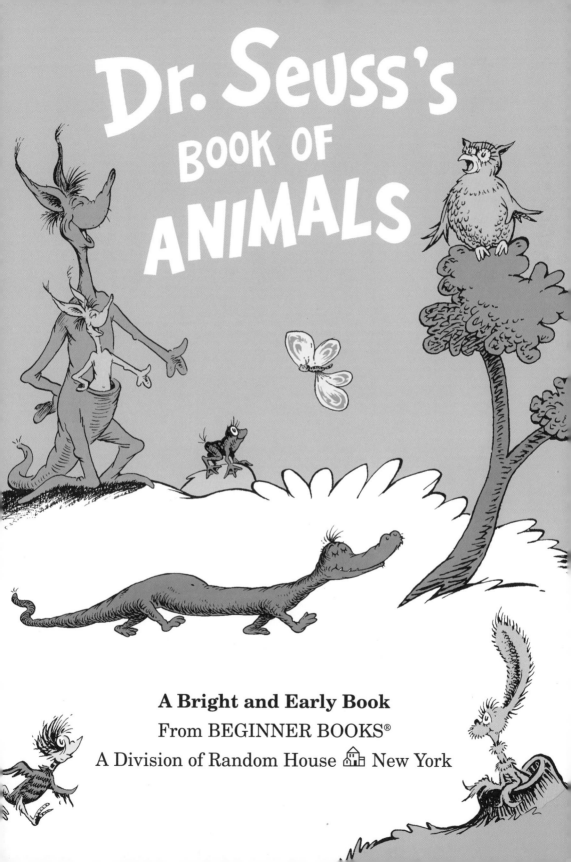

Dr. Seuss's
BOOK OF
ANIMALS

A Bright and Early Book
From BEGINNER BOOKS®
A Division of Random House 🏠 New York

Visit us on the Web!
Seussville.com
rhcbooks.com

Educators and librarians, for a variety of teaching tools, visit us at
RHTeachersLibrarians.com

Library of Congress Cataloging-in-Publication Data
is available upon request.
ISBN 978-1-5247-7055-6 (trade) — ISBN 978-1-5247-7070-9 (lib. bdg.)

MANUFACTURED IN CHINA
10
First Edition

We see animals
all around,
in the sky
and on the ground.

We see a dog.
We see a cat.
We see fish,
thin and fat.

Horse,

cow,

pig,

goat.

Even a crow
in hat and coat.

We see turtles
up in trees.

An animal with two feet.

An animal with four.

An animal with eight feet.

An animal with more!

Some have big teeth.

Some have small.

And some do not
have teeth at all.

This one has feathers.

This one has fuzz.

This one is a
Yuzz-a-ma-Tuzz.

Some animals are shaggy.

Some animals are waggy.

Some are even
ziggy-zaggy!

This one has stripes.

This one has spots.

This one has horns.

This one has knots.

Some live inside.

Some live out.

Some like to smile.

Some like to pout.

This one works hard.

This one is lazy.

This one's mother
is called Mayzie.

Some sleep in beds.

Some sleep in nests.

Some are called pets.

Some are called pests.

Bear and donkey.

Lion and snail.

Mouse and monkey.

Rabbit and whale.

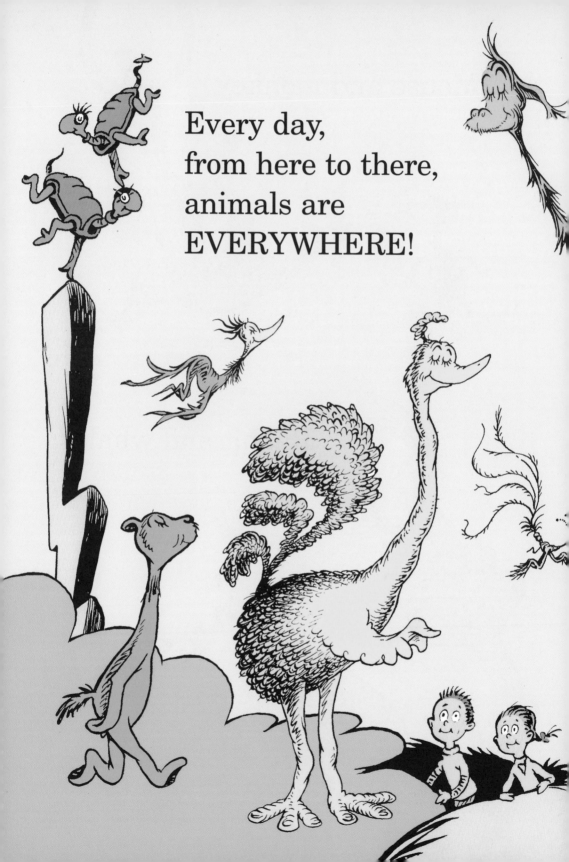

Every day,
from here to there,
animals are
EVERYWHERE!